Praise for The Cat Mummy

'Extraordinarily good at getting inside what worries children . . . a wonderful read and Nick Sharratt's drawings are wittily tender' *Independent*

'A touching and sad situation that is dealt with with a light touch that never trivialises the emotions' *Bookseller*

'Managing to be both hilarious and poignant, *The Cat Mummy* is another sure-fire hit' *Scotsman*

'Loss of a loved one is dealt with lightly and gently' *Financial Times*

'For those aged eight and over you couldn't do better than *The Cat Mummy* . . . the funny, touching tale of Verity whose mum died the day she was born and who doesn't realise how much she loves her do-nothing cat until Mabel disappears. As always, Wilson hits every button' *Express on Sunday*

'Follows the formula that has brought Wilson millions of fans: a big worry explored in the idiom of the young, with a reassuring resolution' *Sunday Times*

Also available by award-winning author,
Jacqueline Wilson

Published in Doubleday/Corgi Yearling Books:

BAD GIRLS

THE BED AND BREAKFAST STAR

BURIED ALIVE!

THE CAT MUMMY

CLIFFHANGER

THE DARE GAME

DOUBLE ACT
Winner of the Smarties Prize,
Winner of the Children's Book Award

GLUBBSLYME

THE ILLUSTRATED MUM
Winner of the Guardian Children's Fiction Prize

THE LOTTIE PROJECT

THE MUM-MINDER

THE STORY OF TRACY BEAKER

THE SUITCASE KID
Winner of the Children's Book Award

VICKY ANGEL

Published in Doubleday/Corgi children's books,
for older readers:

DUSTBIN BABY

GIRLS IN LOVE

GIRLS UNDER PRESSURE

GIRLS OUT LATE

Jacqueline Wilson

THE CAT MUMMY

Illustrated by Nick Sharratt

Corgi Yearling Books

To Nancy (who loves cats)

THE CAT MUMMY
A CORGI YEARLING BOOK: 0 440 86416 X

PRINTING HISTORY
Doubleday edition published 2001
Corgi Yearling edition published 2002

1 3 5 7 9 10 8 6 4 2

Set by Phoenix Typesetting, Ilkley, West Yorkshire.

Corgi Yearling Books are published by Transworld Publishers,
61– 63 Uxbridge Road, London W5 5SA,
a division of The Random House Group Ltd,
in Australia by Random House Australia (Pty) Ltd,
20 Alfred Street, Milsons Point, Sydney, NSW 2061, Australia,
in New Zealand by Random House New Zealand Ltd,
18 Poland Road, Glenfield, Auckland 10, New Zealand
and in South Africa by Random House (Pty) Ltd,
Endulini, 5a Jubilee Road, Parktown 2193, South Africa

Made and printed in Great Britain by
Cox & Wyman Ltd, Reading, Berkshire.

CHAPTER ONE

Mabel

Do you have any pets? My best friend Sophie had got four kittens called Sporty, Scary, Baby and Posh. My second-best friend Laura has a golden Labrador dog called Dustbin. My sort-of-boyfriend Aaron has got a dog too, a black mongrel called Liquorice Allsorts, though he gets called Licky for short. My worst enemy Moyra has got a boa constrictor snake called Crusher. Well, she says she has. I've never been to her house so I don't know if she's telling fibs.

I think Sophie is ever so lucky. I love going round to her house to play with her kittens. They're so sweet, the way they scamper around everywhere. Sophie's mum gets cross sometimes because they knock things over and they've pulled off all the curtain cords but the kittens don't care a bit when she wags her finger at them. The only thing they're the slightest bit frightened of is a little clockwork frog. They used to run away from it but now Scary is getting quite bold and dares stretch out a paw to try to catch it. I could play with Sophie's kittens all day long.

I've been to tea at Laura's house too and made friends with Dustbin. He's a cream dog with big dark shiny eyes and if you hold out your hand he'll shake paws with you. I know exactly why he's called Dustbin. He eats all the time! He's meant to be on a diet as he's getting very plump but he's forever on the scrounge. He especially likes crisps. He even licks out the bag.

Aaron's dog Licky is great at licking too. Aaron takes Licky up to the park after school. My gran and Aaron's mum sit on the bench and have a good gossip and play with Aaron's little sister Aimee and we take Licky for a run.

Then we go on the roundabout and Licky sits on Aaron's lap and barks like crazy because he's having so much fun. Then sometimes if we nag and plead enough my gran or Aaron's mum will buy us a whippy ice-cream from the van at the park gate. Aaron always shares his ice-cream with Licky. It's not really fair on

Aaron so I tried sharing my cone with Licky too, but Gran stopped me. She whispered that I mustn't, because of dog germs. My gran has a bit of a germ fixation. She's not very keen on pets. Apart from Mabel.

I don't know what she'd make of Moyra's pet snake, Crusher. I don't know what *I'd* make of Crusher either. I'm not that keen on snakes actually. Moyra sits behind me at school and today she leant forwards and shot out her arm and wrapped it right round my neck and whispered, 'Watch out, Verity, here comes Crusher!'

I *knew* it was only Moyra, and I'm pretty certain Crusher doesn't even exist – but I still screamed. Everyone giggled. Moyra practically wet herself she laughed so much. Miss Smith didn't tell me off for screaming. She didn't tell Moyra off either. She just raised her lovely black eyebrows and said, 'Settle down, girls'.

I love Miss Smith. She's a new teacher, the nicest we've ever had. I hate Moyra. If there really is a Crusher I hope he wakes up one morning and takes a good look at Moyra's beady eyes and twitchy nose, mistakes her for a giant mouse, and GOBBLES HER UP.

I certainly wouldn't want a snake for a pet, but at least it would be something exciting to boast about.

I have a pet. She is a tabby cat called Mabel. I love her dearly. But she is very, very, very *boring*. She doesn't do anything. She just sleeps. Sometimes I leave her curled up on my bed when I go to school and when I come home there she still is, in exactly the same position. She doesn't go out at night and run round having wild encounters with big bad tom cats. Not my Mabel.

She stays indoors, dozes all evening, and then sleeps all night, back on my bed. She likes to lie on my feet like a live hot-water bottle.

She's about as playful as a hot-water bottle too. I can't believe she was ever a cute little kitten like Sporty, Scary, Baby and Posh. You could run a clockwork frog right *over* Mabel and she wouldn't budge. She's never stalked or killed anything in her life. She doesn't know that's the way cats are supposed to hunt food. She is happy to amble into the kitchen and wait for Gran to open her tin of Whiskas. It's the only exercise she takes all day.

Gran says I've got to remember Mabel is very, very old. Mabel has been very, very old ever since I can remember. She was my mum's cat.

I haven't got a mum. She died the day I was born. That's almost all I know. Gran still can't talk about Mum without her eyes going watery. Even *Grandad* cries. So I don't talk about my mum because I don't want to upset them.

I've got a dad but I don't see him all that often because he's left for work before I get up and he's nearly always still at work when I go to bed. I once heard Gran say my dad is married to his job. Just so long as he doesn't marry a real lady. I definitely don't want a stepmother.

I've read all about stepmothers in fairy stories. They don't have a good image. Laura's got a step*dad* and she certainly doesn't think much of him. He's the one who put poor Dustbin on a diet. He even suggested Laura's *mum* should go on a diet and made her upset about having a big bottom – which she can't help.

Thank goodness Dad doesn't seem interested in any ladies, with big or little bottoms. He hardly ever talks about Mum but he once said she was the loveliest woman in the whole world and no-one could ever replace her. This was a great relief.

I love my dad. He sometimes takes me out for treats on Saturdays, just him and me. For my last birthday he took me all the way on the train to Paris and Disneyland, which was fantastic – *and* he bought me a giant Minnie Mouse doll. I have her in my bed every night. It gets a bit crowded with Mabel as well.

People are sometimes sorry for me because

11

I haven't got a mum. Sophie once put her arms round me and said it must be so awful. I was bad then and made myself look so sad that Sophie would be specially sweet to me, but I really don't mind a bit not having a mum. I don't miss her because I never knew her. The only time *I* get upset is when we go to visit my mum's grave. It's very pretty, with a white headstone, and the words *Beloved Wife and Daughter* in curly writing. Gran always arranges freesias in a little vase. They're my mum's favourite flowers. I can't help thinking

about my poor mum underneath the pink and yellow flowers and the white headstone in the dark, dirty earth. There are worms. I hate thinking about my mum being buried.

I try to imagine her alive instead. I'll tell you a very private secret. I sometimes talk about my mum to Mabel, because Mabel doesn't ever get upset.

I talk and talk and talk about my mum. Mabel listens. When she's not asleep.

CHAPTER TWO

Where's Mabel?

When I got home from school I ran into the hall and stepped straight into this little mess of cat sick.

'Y-u-c-k!'

I was wearing open-toed sandals, which made it a *lot* worse. I hopped around going, 'Yuck Yuck Yuck' and Gran sighed and hurried me into the kitchen and got a bowl of water and a cloth and some disinfectant.

Mabel was dithering at the end of the hall, hanging her head.

'Honestly, Mabel! Why do you have to throw up right where I'm going to walk in it? What have you been eating, you naughty cat? You're disgusting!'

Mabel drooped and slunk away.

'Yes, you jolly well should be ashamed,' I said.

'Don't be too hard on Mabel, Verity,' said Gran. 'I don't think she's very well. That's the second time she's been sick – and she's had a little accident too.'

'Mabel's always having little accidents,' I said. She's so lazy she doesn't amble over to her litter tray in time.

'Mabel isn't getting any younger, you know,' said Gran.

'*You're* not getting any younger, Gran, but you don't sick up your food or do little wees all over the place,' I said, giggling.

'You cheeky baggage,' said Gran, pretending to give me a smack on the bottom.

She laughed, but she still looked a bit worried. My tummy clenched.

'Gran, there's nothing *seriously* wrong with Mabel, is there?' I asked. 'She has just got a little tummy upset, hasn't she?'

Gran hesitated. 'I hope so. I think she's just getting older, dear, like I said.'

'Maybe we should take her to the vet's?'

'I'm not sure there's much they can do for her.'

My tummy clenched tighter.

'But she will be all right, won't she, Gran?' I said. 'I mean . . . she's not going to die or anything?'

I felt myself blushing as if I'd said a really rude word. We hardly ever say words like 'die' or 'death' in my family.

'Well . . .' said Gran, swallowing. 'We've all got to pass away at some time.'

'But not for ages and ages. Mabel isn't going to die *soon*, is she?'

Gran didn't answer properly. She just wriggled her shoulders. 'Shall I make some of my special home-made lemonade? And then maybe you'd like to watch television?'

Gran only makes her lemonade on special days and she usually nags me *not* to watch television. She likes me to read a book or draw a picture or play in the garden.

I started to feel panicky. Gran seemed to think that Mabel might be going to die soon. It sounds so silly but I'd never ever thought about Mabel *dying*. I knew she was old but I sort of assumed she'd stagger on for ever on her soft spreading paws.

I was starting to feel really, really mean for scolding poor Mabel. I wanted to give her a big cuddle and say sorry.

'Back in a minute, Gran,' I said, and I went charging upstairs to my bedroom, Mabel's usual lurking spot.

17

My bed was empty. Well, Minnie Mouse was lying there with her yellow heels sticking up at an angle – but no Mabel.

'Where's Mabel?' I said, tossing Minnie onto the floor.

I looked underneath my bed. Mabel might be really embarrassed about being sick on the hall carpet. She'd hidden underneath my bed in the past. But she wasn't there now.

'Mabel?' I called. 'Where are you, Mabel?'

I looked all round my bedroom. I searched

through the toys and clothes on the carpet. I looked on the windowsill behind the curtain. There was no sign of her anywhere.

I went to look in Gran and Grandad's bedroom. Though Gran always kept their door shut to stop Mabel exploring, Mabel had long ago learnt the knack of nudging it sharply with her hip so that the catch sprang open. I looked on the bed, the rug, the rocking chair, even under the dressing table.

I looked in the bathroom although Mabel detests water and shrieks if I splash her when she noses in and I'm having a bath.

I went charging downstairs and into the kitchen. Gran was stirring her lemonade.

'Gran, I can't find Mabel!'

'She's not on your bed? Though I must say it's not a very hygienic habit, especially if Mabel's poorly. We don't want her being sick on your bed now, do we?'

I wanted Mabel so badly I wouldn't have cared.

'Where *is* she, Gran?'

'What about the living room?'

One of Mabel's favourite snoozing places is the rug in front of the fire. The fire isn't on during the summer but Mabel doesn't seem to notice. She lies there as if she's toasting herself, first lying on one side, then after a little yawn and stretch, settling down to give the other side a turn. I sometimes sit on the chair by the fire and gently rest my bare feet on Mabel's back. She feels like my big furry slipper.

But she wasn't on the rug, though there were cat hairs in a Mabel shape to show she'd had a little lie-down since Gran vacuumed this morning. Mabel wasn't in the chairs or on the sofa or under the table. She wasn't anywhere at all.

'Gran, I can't find her!'

'Mabel?' Gran called. 'Puss puss puss! Come on, old lady. Ma-bel!'

Mabel didn't come.

'I wonder if she's in the garden?' said Gran. 'Here's your lemonade anyway, Verity. And a chockie bickie.'

Gran is the loveliest gran ever, but like all grans she often treats me like a baby. Chockie bickie! That's the way you talk to really *little* kids.

I ate the chocolate biscuit in two bites, drained the lemonade in the glass, and then dashed off to search the garden for Mabel.

She can get out from her cat flap in the back door, but recently she's stayed indoors. She had a worrying encounter with another cat who pounced on her. It was the big ginger tom from up the road. He didn't really do her any harm and I managed to chase him away, but Mabel went all quivery for ages afterwards.

She hasn't set one paw in the garden since.

I still searched it high and low. Grandad searched it too when he came home. Then he said he'd have a look round all the streets for her.

'I want to go with you, Grandad,' I said.

Gran and Grandad didn't think this a good idea. They wouldn't say why at first. I pestered them.

'Something sad might have happened to Mabel, darling,' Gran said eventually. 'We wouldn't want you to see and be upset.'

'What sort of something?' I asked – though I knew.

'Mabel might have been run over, dear. She's getting very old and slow, and I don't think she can see too well,' said Gran.

'But I need to help Grandad look for her! What if she *has* been hurt? I can't stand thinking of Mabel in pain, all lost and frightened.'

'Grandad will do his best to find her, Verity,' said Gran.

But Grandad came back home shaking his head. There was still no sign of Mabel anywhere.

'I want her so much!' I said, and I started to cry.

This time I was glad Gran treats me like a baby. She sat me on her lap and rocked me and Grandad read me a story. I stopped crying – but it didn't stop me aching for Mabel.

I was still wide awake when Dad came home from work. He put his head round my bedroom door, and then sat on my bed while I had another cry.

'What's happened to Mabel, Dad? She can't have disappeared. She never goes wandering off. Not far, anyway. She isn't anywhere. I've searched and searched.'

'I know, pet. Look, we'll write out a notice about Mabel being missing. I'll do lots of copies on my computer and we'll pin them up all over the neighbourhood.'

'And will we get her back then?'

'I hope so, darling.'

'Do you promise?'

Dad hesitated. 'You know I can't promise, Verity.'

'I want Mabel so much, Dad. I haven't been very nice to her recently. I've moaned at her for being so sleepy and yet I know she can't help it. I'd give anything to have her sleeping here on my bed right now.'

'I know, love.'

'I keep thinking about her. She's maybe crying too . . .'

Dad stayed with me for ages, trying to calm me down. I think I went to sleep for a bit. But then I woke up alone in the dark and I felt for Mabel – and she wasn't there.

I hugged Minnie Mouse instead but she wasn't the same. Nothing could ever replace Mabel. I wished I could hold her in my arms and tell her just how much she meant to me.

CHAPTER THREE

The Ancient Egyptian Cats

I didn't sleep properly that night. Mabel padded in and out of my dreams and whenever I woke up the bed was so cold and empty without her.

I had another search of the house when I got up.

'I've had a good look myself,' said Gran. 'There's no sign of her.'

'Let's open her tin of Whiskas and bang the tin opener about a bit. That *always* makes her come,' I said desperately.

Gran opened the tin. She banged the tin opener lots of times. So did I. We both called for Mabel. But Mabel didn't come.

Grandad had another good look when he went to get the newspapers. No luck.

'Perhaps she's been kidnapped!' I said.

'Darling, nobody would want an old cat like Mabel,' said Gran.

'*I* want her,' I said, and I cried again.

I cried so much that Gran and Grandad got really worried.

'Do try and stop, Verity. You'll make yourself ill,' said Gran. 'Come on, now, you're going to be late for school.'

'Maybe she's not in a fit state for school?' said Grandad.

'No, I'm not in a fit state at all,' I sobbed, hoping that I'd be able to stay off and search for Mabel.

But Gran was firm. I had to go to school no matter what. She stuck the cleaned sandals on my feet and fetched me a clean school dress from the airer.

'Come on, stop that crying now, Verity,' she said, buttoning me into my dress.

She couldn't button my lips though.

'You don't understand, Gran. Don't you *care* that Mabel's missing?'

Gran stopped buttoning.

'I care a great deal,' she said, and her voice suddenly sounded wavery, like a radio not tuned in properly. 'I've known Mabel much longer than you, Verity. I remember when we first got her as a kitten and your mother—' Gran's voice suddenly stopped. There were tears in her eyes.

My tummy clenched so tight I couldn't talk either, but I squeezed Gran's hand to show her I was sorry.

'I'll take you to school today, Verity,' said

Grandad. 'Come on, dear. Leave your gran be for now.'

Gran wasn't making any sound but the tears were running down her cheeks. Silent crying seems more frightening than noisy sobs. I hurried off to school with Grandad, looking in every single garden on the way. I kept stopping to peer underneath cars too just in case Mabel was curled up anywhere.

Grandad gave me a hug at the school gate.

'How about a big smile for Grandad?' he asked. I couldn't even manage a very little smile. Grandad was finding it hard to smile too.

'I *wish* I didn't have to go to school, Grandad,' I said, wondering if he'd weaken and let me go back home with him.

But Grandad said maybe playing with my friends would take my mind off Mabel. I didn't see how he could say that. My mind was going Mabel-Mabel-Mabel like a burglar alarm

and when I went into the classroom and started talking to Sophie and Laura and Aaron the Mabel noise didn't stop. It got louder.

'What's up, Verity?' Sophie asked, putting her arm round me.

'Mabel's missing!' I wailed, and I told her all about it.

Sophie was very comforting. She gave me half her Mars Bar from her lunch box and told me that Sporty and Scary and Baby and Posh's mother once went missing.

'She was gone for ages. She made herself a nest in the garden shed. That's where she had her kittens. Maybe your Mabel's having kittens too?'

'Mabel's much too old to have kittens.'

'Maybe she's just gone off on the scrounge,' said Laura. 'Our dog Dustbin does that. He goes into people's gardens and barks piteously as if he's starving and sometimes they fall for it and feed him.'

'I don't think Mabel would do that. She's been a bit off her food recently,' I said. 'She keeps being sick.' I put my head down on my desk. 'I was horrid to her because I stepped in it, but it wasn't her fault at all. Maybe she's really, really ill.'

'Our Licky is sick lots and lots. He eats grass, the silly boy, like he's got this mad idea he's a sheep. Does your Mabel eat grass?'

'No, she just likes her cat food,' I said, speaking into my desk.

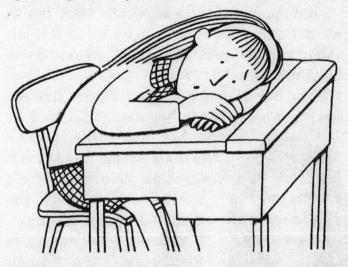

'Good morning, everyone,' said Miss Smith cheerily, coming into the classroom. 'Verity? What's up with you, poppet? Are you sleepy?'

'Mmm,' I mumbled.

'Did you stay up late watching television?'

'No. I couldn't sleep properly.'

'Why's that?' said Miss Smith, coming up to my desk and squatting down beside me.

'I had these bad dreams.'

'Oh dear. Did you tell your mum?'

'My mum's dead,' I said, and I sniffed hard.

Miss Smith looked very upset. 'I'm so sorry,' she said, as if my mum had only died yesterday.

I drooped in my desk while Miss Smith started the lesson, telling us all this stuff about the Ancient Egyptians. We're doing them this term.

Miss Smith looks a bit like an Ancient Egyptian herself with her straight black hair  and her big outlined eyes. We had to do an Ancient Egyptian picture last week. You have to draw all the people looking sideways. Sophie and I got the giggles wondering if the Ancient Egyptians walked about like that.

I didn't feel at all like giggling now.

Moyra gave me a little dig in the back.

'My pet snake Crusher's gone missing too,' she whispered. 'I wonder where he can have got to?'

I knew what was coming. A few seconds later Moyra's arm slithered over my shoulders.

'It's Crusher!' she hissed.

This time I didn't scream. I didn't even flinch.

Moyra tried again, her arm wrapping right round my waist, but I still didn't move.

'Moyra! Leave Verity alone, please,' said Miss Smith.

'You're no fun,' Moyra whispered.

I knew I wasn't any fun. I slumped further down in my chair, thinking about Mabel. I kept remembering how I'd shouted at her for being sick and the sad, shamed way she'd slunk off. I couldn't bear it.

I had to find my hankie quick. I snuffled noisily. Everyone politely took no notice – until I got another poke in the back from Moyra. I thought I was under another Crusher attack, but she whispered, 'Sorry about your cat, Verity. I'm sure she'll come back. We always find Crusher when he goes missing.'

'Moyra!' said Miss Smith.

'I was just saying nice stuff about Verity's cat, Miss Smith!' said Moyra.

'She was, Miss Smith,' I said, blowing my nose.

I'm not always good, but I *am* truthful.

The whole class looked astonished. Moyra and I are famed for our deadly enmity and yet here we were sticking up for each other. Even Miss Smith looked surprised.

'Well, I'm glad to see you two being friendly for once,' she said. 'Still, we're really supposed to be thinking about the Ancient Egyptians, not cats. Though as a matter of fact the

Ancient Egyptians were extremely interested in cats. They kept them as special pets and looked after them very lovingly. If an enemy soldier held a cat as a kind of living armour the Egyptian soldiers wouldn't attack because they were so worried about hurting the cat. They even had a special cat goddess called Bastet. They built a big cat cemetery in her name. When a cat died the owners would shave their eyebrows as a sign of mourning – and very special cats were even made into mummies.'

'Mummies! Wow. Tell us about mummies, Miss Smith,' said Moyra.

I stopped listening. I was saying a prayer to Bastet.

'Please let me find Mabel, oh great cat goddess Bastet,' I whispered. 'Please please please let me find Mabel.'

I had my eyes tightly shut. When I opened them Miss Smith was holding up a picture of

a cat. It looked very odd, long and thin, with no tail or paws, but it had a very distinct cat face and little pointed cat ears. It seemed to be made of cloth rather than fur so I thought it was maybe a toy cat.

'This is a cat mummy,' said Miss Smith, and she told us exactly how the Ancient Egyptians made their poor dead cats into mummies. And this time I listened.

CHAPTER FOUR

The Mabel Mummy

The cat goddess Bastet granted my prayer –
but in the worst way possible.

Gran met me from school. She had make-up
on and she looked smart, but she was still sad.
There was still no sign of Mabel.

'But we've got to remember she's been
missing less than twenty-four hours,' said
Gran.

It seemed like she'd been missing twenty-
four days. No, twenty-four *weeks*. When I went
indoors I wished there was some magic way

I could rewind those twenty-four hours so I could step in the sick in the hall but then pick Mabel up and cuddle her close and tell her how sorry I was that she wasn't feeling well.

But the carpet was clean this time. There was no Mabel hanging her head in the hall.

'I'll make us a little snack,' said Gran, though neither of us was feeling hungry.

I went trailing upstairs to my bedroom. Minnie was sprawled on my bed. I flopped down beside her for a minute. I kicked off my sandals and curled up as if I was going to sleep. Gran came to find me after five minutes.

'Are you having a little nap, Verity? That's a good idea. I'll call you later on for tea, all right?'

Gran tiptoed away. I kept my eyes shut but I couldn't sleep. I felt cold and shivery even though it was a hot day. I didn't want to get right under the covers in my school dress. I suddenly wanted my cosy old winter dressing gown. It was made of blue furry stuff and it had a big black cat head on both pockets.

I got up off the bed and searched through my wardrobe but I couldn't find it at first. It had slipped off the hanger and fallen onto my shoes. I knelt down and rummaged for it. I felt fur . . . real fur.

I gave a little gasp and pulled it out carefully, holding my breath. Mabel was nestled up inside my dressing gown. But there was something terribly wrong with her. Her eyes were half open and she seemed very very stiff.

'Mabel,' I whispered. I shook her gently to try to wake her up. But she couldn't wake up now. My poor darling Mabel was dead.

'Oh Mabel,' I said, and I cradled her in my arms and rocked her to and fro.

I wanted to cry out to Gran but I was so choked up I could barely make a sound. I thought about what would happen next. Mabel would be buried. I couldn't bear the idea of her being smothered under all that dirty earth. Mabel didn't like it out in the garden any more. She'd be so frightened and lonely. And then the worms would get her . . .

'No!' I whispered. 'I'm not going to let them bury you, Mabel, I promise. I'll look after you. I'll keep you safe.'

But I couldn't just leave her tucked up in my dressing gown. She was already starting to look and feel and smell a little strange. I wasn't quite sure how things might progress, but I knew it wouldn't be pleasant. I had to find some way of preserving Mabel.

Then it came to me. It was as if the great cat goddess Bastet had put her holy paw upon me to give the idea. I would make Mabel into a mummy! I wouldn't tell Gran or Grandad or Dad. I knew they might find it too weird – and Gran would probably fuss about hygiene.

I had to do it. It was the perfect way of preserving Mabel for ever. Then I could still hold her in my arms and tell her I loved her and whisper messages to my mum. Mabel would be just like a cat toy, able to stay with me for ever and ever and ever.

So . . . I had to get cracking and turn her into a mummy while Gran thought I was having a nap. I knew the Ancient Egyptians had taken

seventy days but I had less than seventy *minutes*.

I carefully opened up my old dressing gown and spread it out on the bedroom floor. Mabel lay rigidly in the middle. She didn't look well at all. I tried to smooth her fur and mopped her up carefully with a little wad of tissues.

When she was as clean and tidy as I could get her I squatted on my heels, thinking about the next step. I knew what it was. You had to take a piece of wire and stick it in the head and hook out the brain.

Mabel's half-open eyes looked at me. I knew I couldn't possibly do any hooking. I decided to wrap her up whole. I was worried that all her insides might go bad. I had to preserve Mabel under her mummy wrappings.

I knew what the Ancient Egyptians used. It was natron, a special kind of salt. I didn't think you could get natron now. I'd never seen it on the shelves in Sainsbury's. I didn't think ordinary Saxa salt was the right sort of stuff. Then I remembered the big jar of lavender bath salts on the bathroom shelf.

I thought they would be ideal. I crept to the bathroom to check. I saw on the label that they included preservative. Great! Plus they were so sweet-smelling they'd keep Mabel as fragrant as a flower.

I stole back to my bedroom with the jar and tipped the entire contents over Mabel. It looked as if she'd been caught in a lavender snowstorm.

'There, darling,' I whispered, brushing the salts out of her eyes so we could look at each other one last time. 'Now, we'll make you into a mummy.'

Gran kept old sheets at the top of her airing cupboard and only ever got them out when she had to make me a costume for a school play, or when Sophie and I wanted to play ghosts. I took a big sheet and then got cracking with my scissors. I couldn't just wrap the sheet round Mabel like a parcel. I knew you had to make bandages and wrap and wrap and wrap very tightly in a special pattern.

I tried to cut the sheet into neat strips. It was very difficult because I didn't have any decent scissors, just the old blunt-edged ones I used for my scrapbook. Gran had special sharp scissors in the kitchen but I couldn't risk creeping downstairs. I struggled on as best I could

with my own stupid baby scissors until my hands ached, and then I tried ripping bits of sheet.

Time was getting on. I decided I'd better start wrapping with the scraps of sheet I already had. I picked Mabel up tenderly and tried to get her into the right position. I knew I had to straighten her paws and tail so that she would look like a long-necked cat doll when she was finished.

Mabel wouldn't straighten up. She curled up with her paws out and her tail wrapped round herself in her usual going-to-sleep position. She simply wouldn't budge from it. I tried tugging hard but I was terrified her poor old legs might actually snap, and I didn't dare try her tail because it was already so thin and threadbare.

I had no idea how the Ancient Egyptians solved this problem. I decided I simply had to make the best of it and wrapped Mabel up with her paws sticking out and her back all bunched. It wasn't easy. I've never been much good at wrapping Christmas presents. You can't even stick strips of sheet with Sellotape. Every time I got a bit round one part of Mabel another part unravelled. I had to keep tying big knots. Mabel started to look like the most untidy parcel in the world.

I was nearly in tears because I so wanted her to look beautiful and dignified. But as I went on wrapping and wrapping I was able to disguise her shape more – and I was starting to get the hang of doing it neatly. It was like the first time I tried to put my hair into a plait at the back and it was all lop-sided and half the hair hung down, but now I've done it so many times my fingers flash in and out and it ends up as neat as ninepence.

Mabel didn't end up quite as neat as that. As tidy as twopence, more like. But at least she was now officially a mummy.

I got my best set of felt tips and carefully inked green eyes and a pink nose and a red smiley mouth on the sheet over her head. Then I tried to do Egyptian symbols all round her sheeted body. I did that open eye of Horos to protect her and the Ankh sign for good luck. Then I drew lots of things that Mabel liked, a can of catfood and the hearthrug and my bed, with a border of mice and fish and birds to finish it off.

I sat back on my heels when I'd finished and admired Mabel. I needed to keep her in a sarcophagus, the special mummy case. I couldn't think what to use. I tried a shoe box but it wasn't big enough, and it was the wrong shape. I needed something biggish because Mabel was pretty bulky now.

I decided my old duffle bag that I use for swimming might just do as a temporary measure, so I eased Mabel into it as carefully as I could. I put my head in the top of the bag and kissed her wrappings and told her I loved her for ever and ever and ever. Then I gently and reverently placed her in the back of my wardrobe. It wasn't pyramid shape but it was dark and private, so it made a reasonable tomb.

CHAPTER FIVE

Nightmare

'Your little nap did you good, darling,' said Gran, when I went downstairs for tea. 'Mmm! You smell very fresh and pretty!'

'You've got a bit of colour back in your cheeks, poppet,' said Grandad.

They both looked pale and tired but they were trying hard to smile and be cheerful. Gran served us sausage and mash, our favourite – but nobody cleared their plate.

I kept peering at Mabel's dish in the corner of the kitchen. She always had her tea while we ate ours. Sometimes she came scavenging for my leftovers. She particularly liked mashed potato. I had to be careful though. If I gave her too much she was sick.

I thought about the last time poor Mabel was sick and how mean I'd been. My mashed potato got stuck in my throat and I was very nearly sick myself.

Grandad's hand reached out and patted mine. Gran took my plate away and gave me another drink.

'Your dad's going to do his best to come home early tonight,' said Gran.

I wasn't too sure about this. Dad always had to work very, very late. But today he came home just as Gran was clearing the table.

'I'll get your own tea, dear,' she said.

'I'll have it later,' said Dad. 'I thought Verity and I would go out first. I've got heaps of posters about Mabel. We'll pin them up over the neighbourhood. I've even used a photo of her, look, Verity.'

I looked. Dad had done a wonderful poster with a big blown-up picture of Mabel curled up asleep, under the heading HAVE YOU SEEN OUR CAT MABEL?

My heart started banging so hard I thought

it was going to bounce right through my chest and make a mess of my school dress. Dad and I trudged down street after street after street. We pinned Mabel's poster to trees and fences and lamp-posts everywhere we went.

HAVE YOU SEEN OUR CAT MABEL?

'Don't worry, Verity, we'll find Mabel now,' said Dad, taking hold of my hand. 'Someone's bound to see the poster and recognize Mabel and ring our number. She can't have vanished into thin air.'

My heart went bang bang bang. I knew I should tell Dad that Mabel wasn't missing. He had done a hundred posters asking if anyone had seen her. There was only one person in the whole world who knew exactly where she was, entombed in my wardrobe.

I wondered if Dad would understand? I didn't dare risk telling him. You couldn't talk about things like death to Dad. It made him think about Mum. I remembered Gran this morning. It would be even worse if *Dad* started crying.

So I didn't say anything. I was very, very quiet all the way round the neighbourhood and I was very, very quiet when we got home. We were *all* very, very quiet.

I was glad when Gran sent me up to bed. I lay there wide awake. I waited until I heard Gran and Grandad go up to bed. I waited even longer, until I heard Dad go up to bed too. It was a good job I waited, because Dad crept into my room. I closed my eyes tight and lay very still. Dad stood beside my bed a long time. Then he sighed, gently tucked the covers up under my chin, and went out the room.

I still had to wait ages and ages, just to be safe. But when there hadn't been any sound in the house for a long, long time I crept out of bed and very slowly and cautiously opened my wardrobe door. There was a strange smell, half sweet, half sour – bath salts mixed up with the new worrying smell of Mabel.

I decided I mustn't let this put me off. Mabel couldn't help it after all.

I reached into the back of the wardrobe and reverently pulled out the duffle bag. I tried hard but I couldn't pull the Mabel mummy out. I couldn't really see what I was doing in the dark. I had to content myself with inserting one hand into the bag and stroking Mabel's bandages. It was very soothing, very, very soothing . . .

I woke up in the middle of the night to find myself huddled against the wardrobe, the duffle bag clasped to my chest. I wanted to take it back to bed with me, but I didn't dare risk it. I put Mabel back in the wardrobe, shut the door, and then crawled back into bed. I was freezing cold so I wrapped the duvet tightly round me.

I think it was the duvet that gave me the nightmare. I was dead and someone was trying to hook my brains out and I screamed and then they were wrapping me up in bandages, tighter and tighter, and I screamed again. I screamed for someone to come and help me because I was being turned into a mummy . . .

'Verity! Verity, darling, it's Dad. I'm here. Wake up! You're having a nightmare.'

I started sobbing, still thrashing my arms and legs around to free them from the mummy bandages. The duvet fell away and the only thing holding me tightly was Dad.

'Oh, Dad,' I sobbed.

He held me close.

'What's up?' Gran said sleepily, out on the landing. 'Is Verity crying?'

'She had a bad dream,' said Dad. 'She was shouting.'

'What was I shouting?' I said, suddenly scared. 'Did I shout about Mabel?'

Dad didn't answer until Gran had shuffled back to bed.

'I couldn't quite make out what you were saying, pet, but you seemed to be calling for . . . for Mummy.'

I didn't know what to say. My heart was banging again. Dad cleared his throat as if he was about to say more, but no words came out.

There was a deep silence in the dark room.

CHAPTER SIX

Mabel, the Spirit of the Dead

We all overslept in the morning. It was just as
well. Gran noticed all the bath salts were
missing.

'How can they have disappeared?' Gran said,
bewildered.

She asked Grandad if he'd used them. He
said he didn't want to smell like a lavender
bush, thanks very much, so he never used so
much as a sprinkle.

'Verity? *You* didn't use them all up, did you?'
said Gran. 'I know it can't have been your dad.

He only ever has a quick shower.'

'I – I might have used some of them,' I mumbled, running away from Gran into my bedroom. 'Sorry, Gran, I've got to pack my school bag.'

But Gran followed me into my bedroom. She sniffed suspiciously.

'My goodness! I can *smell* the bath salts! What on earth did you do? Tip the whole *jar* in your bath?'

'Please don't be cross, Gran,' I said, frantically shoving my books and PE kit into my school bag.

I shoved a little *too* frantically and the zip jammed. I tugged. I tugged too hard.

'Oh no!'

'Verity! Silly girl! You should have eased the zip. Now look at it! Where's your duffle bag? You'd better take your stuff in that.'

'No! No, I . . . I can't. I don't like my duffle bag. No-one takes duffle bags to school any more. This bag's still fine, Gran. I'll pin it. Oh please, let's hurry, we're *late*.'

I dodged round Gran, clutching my broken bag in my arms. I hoped she'd have forgotten all about the bath salts by the time school was over.

We couldn't forget about poor Mabel. There were all the posters on every tree and fence, her sweet face peering at us plaintively.

'I'd give anything in the whole world for Mabel to be safe and sound somewhere,' Gran muttered. 'I'll stay in all day just in case anyone phones with news of her.'

'Oh Gran,' I said.

I trailed into school, feeling terrible. The bell had already gone but Miss Smith didn't tell me off when I sidled into the classroom.

'How are you today, Verity? Any more bad dreams?' she asked.

I nodded. 'Horrible nightmares.'

'Oh dear,' she said, and she patted my shoulder as I went past.

Sophie and Laura and Aaron were all extra-nice to me. Even *Moyra* was nice. She offered to share her sweets with me at break-time. She had two big wiggly green jelly snakes.

'You can have one if you want, Verity,' she said.

I said I wasn't very hungry, thank you. She did tease a bit then, shaking a snake right in my face and asking if I was frightened of *sweets* – but Aaron elbowed her out the way and asked if I was going to the swings after school. Laura told me her next-door neighbour had heard a cat mewing in the night and it might have been Mabel. Sophie said if Mabel didn't ever come back maybe I'd like Sporty or Scary or Baby or Posh because her mum said they couldn't keep all the kittens.

I thanked Aaron but said I didn't really feel like a trip to the swings. I thanked Laura and said I didn't think it could have been Mabel. I thanked Sophie and said I loved Sporty and Scary and Baby and Posh . . . but they could never ever replace my Mabel.

I thought about Mabel most of the morning. I got a lot of my sums wrong. But after dinner Miss Smith gave another lesson on the Ancient Egyptians, and I started to listen properly. She held up this rather scary-looking jackal mask and asked who wanted to try it on and be Anubis, the god of the dead. Moyra nearly wet herself she was so desperate to be chosen. Miss Smith let everyone take turns while she told us all about the Ancient Egyptians' beliefs about death.

They were sure the spirit left the body but might come back to it later on. That's why they thought it very important to preserve the bodies. They needed to be kept in spic and span condition in case the spirit paid a visit.

I felt relieved that I had done my very best for Mabel. I decided to leave the wardrobe door ajar so that Mabel's spirit could waft out and go for a walk round all her old haunts whenever she felt like it.

'Can you see the spirit, Miss Smith?' I asked.

'Well, the Ancient Egyptians painted pictures of the spirits of the dead, and they always drew them like big birds.'

I blinked at the idea, trying to imagine Mabel with wings. She'd look a little odd but I knew she'd enjoy being able to fly. She could swoop straight out the house and up over the rooftops and save her poor old paws. She could have such fun chasing all the sparrows and perch in the tallest tree and never ever get stuck.

Miss Smith showed us all a picture of Anubis weighing a heart on the scale to see if it balanced with the feather of truth so that the mummy could be made immortal.

'So the mummies live for ever and ever and you can be together in the afterlife?' I said, imagining Mabel and me flying hand in paw for ever.

Miss Smith was looking at me worriedly.

'It's just what the Ancient Egyptians believed, Verity,' she said gently.

'But we can believe it too,' I said.

'Well . . .' said Miss Smith uncertainly.

'*I* believe it,' said Moyra. 'I love the Ancient Egyptians. Show us those snaky demons in that Dead Book, Miss Smith. They're brilliant!'

Miss Smith started to tell everyone about the serpent demons and the crocodile monsters. Everyone got very excited. I didn't join in. I thought about Mabel instead.

I decided I needed to fill her wardrobe tomb with some special toys and a tin or two of Whiskas. She once had her own catnip mouse but it had got lost somewhere. I didn't have any other sort of mice, apart from Minnie, and she was much too big.

At the end of lessons Miss Smith called me back.

'Verity? Can I have a little word?'

I thought she was going to tell me off for not paying attention. I got flustered and forgot about the broken zip on my school bag. Everything fell out with a thump and a clatter as I made my way up to Miss Smith's desk.

'Oh dear,' said Miss Smith. She helped me collect up my stuff. 'It's not your day today, is it, Verity?'

'No, Miss Smith.'

'Verity . . . you seem rather unhappy at the moment,' Miss Smith said gently.

I hung my head.

'And you're obviously not sleeping very well.'

'I'm sorry, Miss Smith.'

'It's not your fault, poppet. I'm not telling you off. I just want to try to help.' She paused. 'I know things must be very sad at home at the moment.'

I looked up. Someone must have told her about Mabel.

'Perhaps . . . perhaps you could try talking about your mum with your dad? Or maybe your gran?'

I blinked at Miss Smith, wondering why she'd suddenly switched to talking about my *mum*?

'I can't talk about my mum,' I said. My throat went tight because the only person I could ever talk to about Mum was Mabel.

'Can I go now, Miss Smith?' I whispered. I didn't want to burst into tears in front of her.

I ran off quickly before she said yes. I

thought I heard her calling me, but I didn't stop.

Gran was waiting at the gate, looking anxious.

'Where have you been, Verity? Aaron and the others came out ten minutes ago. Did Miss Smith keep you in?'

'Oh, she just wanted to talk to me for a bit,' I said, hurrying along beside Gran. 'Can I have an ice-cream?'

'No, dear. And don't try to change the subject! What did she want to talk to you about?'

'Oh . . . nothing.'

Gran sighed.

'Are you in any trouble?'

'No, Gran.'

'Verity? Are you telling me the truth?'

I managed to look Gran straight in the eye. 'Yes, Gran.'

CHAPTER SEVEN

Mabel the Mummy

I try very hard to tell the truth. That's what my name Verity means. You look it up. It's Latin for truth.

I can be as naughty as the next person but I try not to tell lies. However . . . it was getting harder and harder with this Mabel-mummy situation. I hadn't been *completely* truthful about the missing bath salts, or my duffle bag, or my conversation with Miss Smith. But I hadn't told any actual downright lies. Yet.

As soon as I got home I went charging up

to my bedroom to have a private word with Mabel. I shut my bedroom door and put a chair against it just in case. Then I opened my wardrobe.

I wished I hadn't.

The smell was a lot worse. The bath salts weren't doing their work. Mabel smelt as if she was in dreadful distress and needed cleaning up. I felt I should ease her out of the duffle bag and attend to her, but when I undid the drawstring at the top the smell was suddenly so overpowering that I reeled backwards. I shoved Mabel in her bag to the very back of the wardrobe and closed the door quick.

I sat on my heels wondering what on earth to do. I wondered and wondered and wondered.

'What are you up to, Verity?' Gran called. 'Are you having another nap?'

'No, Gran. Coming!' I said hastily and shot downstairs.

I didn't want to risk her coming up to my bedroom when the smell had seeped so strongly out of the wardrobe. The smell seemed to have stuck to me too because Gran wrinkled her nose when I went into the kitchen.

'Whatever's that awful smell, darling?'

'What smell, Gran?' I said, trying to look as wide-eyed and innocent as possible.

'Verity . . . ?' Gran paused, looking embarrassed. 'You haven't had a little accident, have you?'

'No, Gran!' I said indignantly.

Gran was still looking at me very strangely.

'I think you'd better pop off and have a bath anyway, dear – and change your dress too.' Gran paused. 'I've bought some new bath salts but please be very careful with them this time. Only tip a little into your bath.'

So I had a bath and felt a lot fresher. But the clean clothes were a BIG problem. They were hanging in my wardrobe. When I opened the door a crack and smelt them I knew I couldn't possibly put any of them on.

I started to panic. I'd have to try to creep downstairs with all my clothes in the middle of the night and put them in the washing machine. But what was I going to do *now*?

I ended up putting on my old fairy costume which I found screwed up at the bottom of my toy box. I hadn't worn it for a couple of years. It was much too short and much too tight. I felt a perfect fool, but at least it only smelt of old teddy bears.

Gran looked astonished when I lumbered

downstairs, wings flapping, net skirts barely covering my knickers.

'What on earth have you got that fairy frock on for, Verity?'

'I wanted to play fairies, Gran. Please let me,' I said, and I swooped about, pretending to be a soppy little fairy.

'What a lovely fairy! Can I have a wish?' said Grandad, coming in from the garden.

I had to keep on and on playing fairies. I was still flitting about granting magic wishes when Dad came home – early again, in time for tea.

'Is that the latest fashion?' Dad said warily, peering at me.

'Oh Dad, don't be silly,' I said. 'I'm being a fairy, right?'

I did a daft pointy-toe dance to demonstrate.

Dad and Gran and Grandad had a muttered conference while I twirled.

'She seems to have perked up astonishingly.'

'She didn't even ask if there were any phone calls about Mabel.'

'I came home early in case she wanted to do another search of the neighbourhood, but it seems a shame to suggest it now.'

It was easier if they all thought me a heartless baby who'd forgotten all about Mabel, but I hated having to act the part, especially when Gran pandered to me and gave me an extra fairy cake at tea.

We were all still sitting at the table when the doorbell rang. Gran went to answer it and came back into the living room . . . with Miss Smith!

'I'm so sorry! I've interrupted you when you're having your meal,' said Miss Smith.

'Not at all! We've finished anyway. Let me get you a cup of tea or coffee, Miss Smith,' said Dad, leaping up.

'I'll do it, dear,' said Gran. She doesn't like anyone helping her in the kitchen.

Grandad was looking at me, eyebrows raised.

'Is our Verity in a spot of bother at school, Miss Smith?' he asked.

Gran frowned.

'Verity? What have you been up to? Go and put a clean school frock on, dear. Whatever will Miss Smith think seeing you in your funny fairy outfit?'

'Oh no, please. You look sweet, Verity,' said Miss Smith. 'Don't worry, Verity's not in any trouble at all. I just came round because Verity dropped her purse. It fell out of her school bag and rolled under a desk. I brought it round in case you were worried about it.'

'How kind of you,' said Dad. 'Say thank you, Verity.'

'I knew it was silly taking that broken bag to school. You'll take your duffle bag tomorrow,' said Gran.

'I can't!'

They all looked at me.

'I mean . . . I lost my duffle bag.'

'Don't be silly, Verity, of course you haven't lost it,' said Gran. 'And *do* go and put some decent clothes on, dear.'

'I don't think I've got any clean clothes, Gran.'

Gran frowned at me.

'Verity! What's the matter with you? There's at least ten different clean outfits hanging in your wardrobe. Now go and put something on *at once!*'

Gran doesn't often get cross, but when she uses that tone you can't argue with her.

I looked desperately at Grandad.

'Can't I stay in my fairy frock, Grandad?' I pleaded.

Grandad tutted at me. 'Do as Gran says, darling,' he said.

I looked at Dad.

'Upstairs, Verity. Quick sharp,' said Dad.

So I went upstairs, very very slowly. I stopped to listen halfway up.

'That's not like our Verity. She's usually such a good little girl, does as she's told and never any arguing.'

'Of course she's had a worrying time, lately.'

'Has she seemed upset at school, Miss Smith?'

'Well yes, she hasn't been her usual self at all. I agree, she's generally a lovely cheery little girl, a total joy to teach. But of course when she's had such a devastatingly terrible bereavement to deal with—'

'Bereavement?' said Dad. 'We don't know for sure that Mabel's dead.'

'We've done our best to advertise.'

'She might come back yet. It's a bit soon to give up hope – though she's never run away before.'

'But . . . I thought . . . Verity said . . . so her mum's left home?' said Miss Smith.

'Her *mum*?' said Gran. 'No no, my daughter passed away long ago.'

'When our little Verity was born,' said Grandad.

'Has Verity been talking about her mum at school, Miss Smith?' said Dad. 'I think she's been dreaming about her. It's been worrying me a lot. Perhaps you can help us. We've never been very good at talking about it—'

'It's too upsetting,' said Gran.

'Of course she didn't ever know her mum,' said Grandad.

'I see,' said Miss Smith, though it was clear she didn't. 'So . . . who is Mabel?'

'Oh! That's our cat,' said Dad.

I gave a moan. Gran came whipping outside into the hall.

'Verity! Are you hanging about on the stairs listening to us? I told you to go and get some sensible clean clothes on!'

'I can't, Gran!'

'Whatever's the matter with you today?' said Gran crossly. 'Why are you showing me up in front of Miss Smith? And what have you been *saying* to her?'

I hung my head, unable to explain. Gran sighed. She took hold of my arm and started pulling me up the stairs.

'No, Gran! Please! Don't!' I whimpered, realizing where we were heading.

Gran tugged me into the bedroom. She stopped to get her breath. She sniffed.

'What *is* that smell?'

'I . . . I'm not sure,' I said, which was the biggest lie yet, because I was surer than sure.

My eyes swivelled towards the wardrobe. So did Gran's. She stepped towards it.

'Don't!'

But she did. She flung the door open – and then reeled backwards, choking.

'Oh my goodness! What on *earth* . . . ?' She bent down and saw the duffle bag at the back.

'There's your duffle bag! Is that where the awful smell is coming from? Don't say you've left your wet swimming things in there all this time?'

She seized the duffle bag, pulled it out into

the open, undid the top . . . and tipped the contents onto my carpet.

Then Gran screamed and screamed and screamed. Dad came running. Miss Smith came running. Grandad came hobbling.

Gran went on screaming for a long, long time. Even after she was downstairs and trembling in her armchair and Miss Smith had poured her a cup of strong sweet tea, Gran still made little gaspy sounds.

Dad and Grandad made loud gagging sounds as they shovelled poor Mabel and her duffle bag into a big black plastic rubbish sack and carted her outside into the garden. Then they washed and washed and washed.

I wept until the front of my stupid fairy frock was sodden.

Miss Smith made a fresh pot of tea when Dad and Grandad came back.

'I'm so sorry,' Gran gasped. 'I should have made the tea. Whatever must you think of us?'

'I reckon you got more than you bargained for when you brought our Verity's purse back!' said Grandad.

'Verity?' said Dad.

They all looked at me. I wept harder.

'Don't cry so, pet. I'm not cross. I'm just . . . puzzled. *Why* did you hide Mabel in your duffle bag? And why did you wrap her up like that?'

'It was bandages. Did you think it would make her better?' said Grandad.

'Bandages!' said Miss Smith.

She looked at me. I looked at her.

'Oh dear, oh dear!' said Miss Smith. 'You tried to make Mabel into a cat mummy!'

CHAPTER EIGHT

Mabel R.I.P.

It all came out. Gran was very upset, wondering how I could have done such a silly, shameful thing. Grandad started spluttering with laughter. Dad was fussed because I hadn't said anything the moment I'd found Mabel.

'I *couldn't*,' I shouted. 'She was dead. We don't talk about anyone being dead because we all get upset and dead people have to be buried and I couldn't bury Mabel because she's frightened of outdoors and she'd hate to be buried under the dirty earth with all the worms.'

I thought they'd all be cross with me for shouting like that. Not a bit of it! They looked shocked. Then they all started being very *kind*. Gran sat me on her lap and Grandad said he'd donate his special toolbox as a coffin and Mabel would stay safe inside. Miss Smith said I could maybe paint the toolbox with Egyptian signs so that it would be like a special mummy case. She said the very first Ancient Egyptians used very similar wooden boxes. If I painted big Egyptian eyes on the side of the box then this would mean Mabel could look out, and I could also paint a special door so her spirit could get in and out of the coffin.

'A special little cat-flap door,' I said, blowing my nose. 'That's right, Verity,' said Miss Smith, giving me a hug. It was as if she'd stopped being my teacher and was now a member of my family.

Dad had a little private word with her. I couldn't hear much until right at the end. Miss Smith

said I was her special favourite in her class. She really did! I wish I could tell Sophie and Laura and Aaron. I especially wish I could tell Moyra. But I know it's a secret. And I'd hate it if Miss Smith told *my* secret to the whole class.

After Miss Smith went Gran started a very, very long session with disinfectant and scrubbing brush in my wardrobe while all my clothes whirled round and round in the washing machine. Grandad took all his tools out of the toolbox and cleaned it up and sanded it down so it was smooth for me to paint on.

Dad helped me do the painting. It was getting quite late by this time but we all knew Mabel couldn't wait much longer to be buried. I needed to wear something more sombre than a fairy outfit and all my clothes were being washed, so I took another of Gran's old sheets and wrapped it round and

81

round me and secured it with a purple chocolate box ribbon. I looked almost like an Ancient Egyptian myself.

Dad and Grandad went out into the garden with the box. They wouldn't let me come while they were putting Mabel into her new coffin. They wouldn't let me kiss her goodbye. So I went to the hearthrug in the living room where some of Mabel's cat hair still lingered. I curled up very small and kissed the soft spot on the rug where Mabel always put her head.

Then Dad and Grandad called me and I went outside. Mabel was safely entombed in the box. There was still rather a smell wafting around the garden but it couldn't be helped. Dad had already started digging a big hole down by the apple tree at the bottom of the garden. Grandad dug too. I got my old baby spade and dug as well, though I got the sheet a bit muddy. It was getting dark so I couldn't see if there were any worms. It was maybe just as well.

It took *ages* to make the hole big enough. Gran came out and said I should go to bed and Mabel could be buried in the morning now she was safe in her box, but Dad said it was important to have the ceremony now.

At last the hole gaped wide enough for Dad and Grandad to lower Mabel in her box down into it. Grandad let me pick a little bunch of his roses. I scattered the petals on top of Mabel.

'Perhaps you'd like to say something, Verity?' said Dad.

'Dear Mabel, I love you and I'm so sorry I shouted at you. Please be happy in your after-life and fly back and see if you can visit me. You're the best cat in the world and I *wish* I could have preserved you as a proper mummy . . .' I started to cry and couldn't carry on.

'But you will always be preserved in our memory,' said Dad.

Then he trickled a handful of earth onto the petal-strewn box. Grandad did too. They looked at me.

'I wish we didn't have to cover her up,' I said.

'It's like planting a bulb,' said Grandad. 'Mabel will make lots of lovely flowers grow in the Spring.'

I fidgeted. I didn't think Mabel was *remotely* like a bulb. I didn't want her to grow into flowers. I wanted her to grow back into herself

84

so I could cuddle her and love her and keep her for ever.

'Couldn't we just keep her in her box now?' I said.

'*Not* a good idea,' said Grandad.

'We have to make sure she's safe and undisturbed,' said Dad. 'But I know just how you feel, Verity. When . . . when your mum died . . . the burying bit was the hardest of all.' He reached for my hand and held it tight. 'But we have to do it and there's no way of making it better. You're going to miss Mabel terribly. We all are. But gradually it stops hurting quite so badly.'

'Do you still hurt about Mum, Dad?' I whispered.

'A lot of the time, yes. And Gran does. And Grandad. But although I'm sad some of the time I'm also happy too. And you will be as well, I promise. Now let's say goodbye to Mabel.'

'Goodbye Mabel,' I said, and I took a handful of earth and carefully sprinkled it over her.

Then I went back inside while Dad and Grandad covered Mabel up.

Gran was putting another batch of my clothes in the washing machine.

'Honestly!' she said, shaking her head at me. But then she gave me a big hug and made me a mug of hot chocolate because I'd got cold staying out in the garden so long.

My bedroom smelt very strongly of disinfectant when I went up to bed. I looked sadly at the empty wardrobe. I wished I could have kept Mabel as a mummy. I wished she was still alive. I wished I hadn't been mean to her. I felt very sad . . . but I felt peaceful instead of worried.

I didn't tell Sophie or Laura or Aaron what I'd done when I went to school the next morning. I certainly didn't tell Moyra. Sophie asked straight away if Mabel had come back. I took a deep breath.

'Yes. I found her. But she was dead. So we buried her in the garden.'

Sophie put her arm round me. So did Laura. Aaron looked awkward and mumbled that he was very, very sorry. Moyra started asking questions, wondering where I'd found Mabel and what she looked like. She asked if she'd started to go mouldy.

'Shut up,' I said. 'I don't want to talk about it.'

Sophie and Laura and Aaron told Moyra to shut up too. So she did.

I was tremendously relieved that Miss Smith didn't breathe a word about Mabel at school. She didn't single me out in any way or act like I was her special favourite. She was so just-like-any-old-teacher that I started to feel a bit disappointed, but when the bell went for going-home time she asked me to come and see her.

'I wonder why Miss Smith wants you, Verity?' said Sophie.

'I hope she's not cross with you,' said Laura.

'I hope she *is*,' said Moyra.

'I hope she doesn't keep you long. You've got to come up to the park today, you haven't been for *ages*,' said Aaron.

Miss Smith didn't keep me long. She just smiled at me and asked me gently how I was.

'I still feel really bad about Mabel,' I said.

'Of course you do,' said Miss Smith. 'Look, I've found you a book that tells you all about the Egyptian Book of the Dead. It's full of magic spells and prayers for dead people.'

'Is there one for dead cats?' I asked eagerly.

'I'm not sure. Perhaps you can make one up. You could write it out in your best hand-writing and do a special picture of Mabel. Maybe you could make your own little book about her? You could stick in photos and

write about all the happy times you had with
her. It could be a special way of remembering
her for always.'

'I like that idea!' I said. Then I added shyly,
'And I like you, Miss Smith. In fact you've
always been *my* special favourite.'

Miss Smith laughed and went pink and told
me to run along.

I went up to the park with Gran and Aaron and Aaron's mum and baby Aimee and Licky.

We passed some of the Mabel posters on the way. I hung my head and felt sad, but in the park Licky caught this little boy's ball and wouldn't give it back and we all had to play

Chase the Dog and it was such fun that I almost forgot about Mabel.

I remembered her when we got home though. I went back into the garden and knelt by her grave and whispered to her. The earth was packed tight so it didn't look as if her spirit had flown out of the box yet.

Grandad called me to come in but I didn't want to. Grandad came out into the garden and kept me company for a bit. Then Dad got home and came and put his arm round me.

'You've been early three days in a row, Dad!' I said.

'I'm going to try to get away early *every* day now,' said Dad. 'I think we need to spend more time with each other, Verity. You know it's so stupid, I've spent such a long time feeling sad that your mummy died, and yet I should also be feeling so very glad that I've got you.'

He said it as if he'd been rehearsing what to say all the way home from work, but it still sounded good.

He asked if Miss Smith had said anything at school and I told him about doing a book about Mabel.

'That's a wonderful idea! Miss Smith is *so* clever. You're very lucky to have such a lovely teacher, Verity,' said Dad. 'It's Saturday tomorrow, so we'll go shopping for a special notebook for Mabel.'

⟨HAPTER NINE

The Egyptian Book of the Dead Mabel

We ended up buying two special big blank books. One for Mabel. And one for my mum.

'You can do Mabel's book all by yourself, Verity,' said Dad. 'And we'll work on Mummy's book together, just you and me. I want you to know all about her.'

'Don't you mind me talking about her now?'

'I don't mind a bit. I think we should talk. I was silly not to before.'

'Can I talk about her to Gran and Grandad too?'

'Maybe that's not such a good idea. Gran still finds it too sad.'

'Dad, did Miss Smith tell you to talk about my mum?' I asked.

Dad went a bit red.

'Well . . . we did sort of . . . yes, it was really her idea,' he said.

'She has great ideas, doesn't she?' I said. 'I do like her. Do you like her, Dad?'

'Mmm. Yes. I like her a lot,' said Dad, and he went even redder. He smiled. I smiled too.

We worked on our books all weekend.

A BOOK ABOUT MUMMY

This is a picture of Mummy when she was a little girl. She looks just like Verity. (though I wouldn't wear a frock like that!)

Mummy liked reading and dancing and swimming and drawing when she was a little girl. (So do I!)

She always wanted a pet but Gran wasn't too keen. Mummy had to wait till she was grown up and married to Daddy.

Then they had Mabel.
(The best cat in the world.)

Mummy and Daddy wanted to have children very much. This is a picture of Mummy looking very happy because she was expecting a baby. (Me!)

A BOOK ABOUT MABEL

This is my cat Mabel. She was the best cat in all the world and I shall never ever forget her.

Mabel lived for a very long, long time. I didn't know her when she was a kitten. She looks sweet, doesn't she?

You will never guess what! I've got a kitten now!

Sophie and her mum and dad came round on Sunday and said I could choose one of their kittens. I wasn't sure at first. I badly wanted a kitten but it felt as if I was being unfair and disloyal to Mabel.

'I understand, Verity. But loving one cat a great deal doesn't mean you can never ever love another one,' said Dad. 'I should say "yes, please" to a kitten if I were you.'

So I went back to Sophie's house and we spent a long time playing with Sporty, Scary, Baby and Posh.

They were all so *sweet*. Sporty's already started to climb the curtains! Scary is very bold and chases after the clockwork frog. Posh is probably the prettiest and seems to know it, stretching out elegantly as if she's posing. But Baby is the cuddliest.

'You can have whichever one you like,' said Sophie. 'Only I rather hope you won't choose Sporty as she's such a pickle. And Scary's so funny. And Posh just looks so perfect.'

It was no problem at all choosing. I desperately wanted Baby.

So now I have my very own kitten and I love her to bits. I'm going to look after her properly and I shall never ever be cross with her. I hope she lives until long after I'm grown up. But I know one thing. I'll never love Baby *quite* as much as I loved my Mabel . . .